CZECH
TECHNO
& Other Stories
of Music

Other books by Mark Anthony Jarman

POETRY

Killing the Swan

SHORT STORIES

Dancing Nightly in the Tavern
New Orleans Is Sinking
My White Planet
19 Knives
Knife Party at the Hotel Europa

NOVEL

Salvage King, Ya!

TRAVEL

Ireland's Eye: Travels

CZECH TECHNO

& Other Stories
of Music

by Mark Anthony Jarman

anvil press • vancouver

Anvil Press Publishers Inc.
P.O. Box 3008, Station Terminal
Vancouver, B.C. V6B 3X5 CANADA
www.anvilpress.com

LIBRARY AND ARCHIVES CANADA CATALOGUING IN PUBLICATION

Title: Czech techno : and other stories of music / Mark Jarman ; illustrations by Chris Tompkins.
Names: Jarman, Mark Anthony, 1955- author. | Tomkins, Chris, illustrator.
Description: Short stories.
Identifiers: Canadiana 20200290355 | ISBN 9781772141382 (softcover)
Classification: LCC PS8569.A6 C94 2020 | DDC C813/.54—dc23

Cover design and interior illustrations by Chris Tomkins
Interior design by HeimatHouse
Represented in Canada by Publishers Group Canada
Distributed in Canada by Raincoast Books and in the US by Small Press Distribution

The publisher gratefully acknowledges the financial assistance of the Canada Council for the Arts, the Canada Book Fund, and the Province of British Columbia through the BC Arts Council and the Book Publishing Tax Credit.

An irregular series showcasing shorter works by established authors. This may include collections of poetry or prose, critical writing, chapbooks, pamphlets, broadsides, posters and any manner of literary ephemera the editors deem fitting to the series.

PRINTED AND BOUND IN CANADA

To Clarissa with love
and in memory of Billy the cowboy

Table of Contents

CZECH TECHNO

(Hail to That Which Surrounds You)

Beg the bee's forgiveness
As it's falling from your sleeve
— "Let the Devil In," TV on the Radio

I thought she was dead, but she seems very real now, standing by the hedge in her glowing dress. I think we're in Iceland, or Denmark, somewhere seriously lunar and attractive. My wallet is missing, and my cell phone has disappeared. The rest of the band, the collective, is inside bitching at each other about the cost of microphones, and I am pacing outside a mansion's back door.

The mansion is three severe storeys and a steep attic topped by an iron filigree widow-walk high above a river, a yellow river that steps through fieldstone locks and granite walls. And just *there*, this woman I thought dead, in an airy white dress, as if party to a Nordic wedding.

Her e-mail three years ago: *Maybe $20 isn't enough for a phone. I felt sad after our talk and frustrated that I couldn't call back. Just before the phone died I wanted to tell you that I want to pay for the* *flight. It's not that I'm worried about being indebted. I want to see you and don't mind paying.*

These trapped interior waters and this house's infinite green grounds seem utterly familiar. The stone walls and paths and muscular hedges would suit a ruined Irish estate, a Norman abbey — but not necessarily our trance band, our flash-in-the-pan band gone way over the budget, off the rails, spending money that nervous label execs advanced us for recording and now going in the hole, spending wheelbarrows of cash they didn't give us.

Please don't fall in with love with her — she's not really Irish and too rough for tender you.

It's dusk in the yard, or perhaps it is already dawn — we all seek that fond light that finds tresses and secret undergarments, that expensive light — and by the hedge a hesitant blond woman in a cool, confused dress, mystery in her eyes, in her eyes I see devotion and disaster and the name of a good lawyer.

A HONEYSUCKLE HEDGE bordered the south side of my childhood yard, a high hedge tilting over a deep ravine. The same tiny leaves are strewn at this hedge's chicken feet, and I feel I'm back studying that private childhood nook, I'm standing by that exact eroded ravine, except that this new place boasts screaming peacocks with feathered tails like giant Georgian tattoos and I think something tiny inside me has evaporated.

I chalk up this dislocation and desolation to jetlag, to time zones in my brain arguing with each other like my family at the dinner table.

That can't be her after all these years, can it? My eyes are not good and my Buddy Holly Weezer glasses are no longer standing at attention in my breast pocket.

I'm glad you like the tortillas I mailed, which were actually Norwegian lefse. They thought it was the cervix but it's in the uterus. They want to take it out, but I don't know. I know you'll scoff, but I'm going to see a doctor in Mexico.

This ghostly woman at the hedge brings back my lost fiefdom. Winter and we neck on the way home from the bar, fat snowflakes like tiny soft maps and no one else walks the streets: our world alone. A few steps and grasp each other, a few more steps and clasp, our laughter, my fingers tracing her cheekbones, my mouth moving on her throat and ear.

God, it was such fun, even when she slipped on ice and I used that as an excuse to be sure her leg was not hurt. She stood patiently while I crouched and happily ran my hand deep into the small funnel of her skirt to brush snow from her black tights.

This I knew long ago and somehow lost, the trance music stopped, but now, seeing her (*is it her?*), seeing her starts the chain again in my head – ah, I hate that, I wanted to be rid of it, to be done with it all, purged of those hymns to memories that are bad because they are so fucking good, those hymns to misunderstandings, those shadow-box anthems of lost icy street corners and vanished republics, like Fredonia, like Rupert's Land, Van Dieman's Land, Greasy Grass, Vinegar Hill, Desire Trench, like Frippertronics, like Momentik.

LOCALS CLAIM THESE steep ravines opened deep in the earth when Christ was crucified; the Roman soldier jabbed in the spear and the earth opened here in Finland or Iceland or Vineland or wherever we are recording (or failing to record) our pivotal second CD.

All our takeoffs and landings and ground crews and flight crews and fuck yous bleeding into each other under Homeland Security X-rays and electric eyes and glowing taxis like fleet spacecraft flying over strange cobbled lanes laid down in 1506 and where-oh-where is the unique boutique hotel?

And didn't the Lithuanian or Latvian airline lose our amps and we have to rent a PA head and a DAW and a ton of other gear by the minute and insurance won't cover the nut and it's not my fault, but I have a giddy feeling the band wants to oust me. Can they fire me? Why can't I move, do anything?

Dear true friend and tender animal, she once wrote, *I miss us talking; it makes me sad,* she wrote. *If you came, if you were coming in the fall.* To buy time with her gorgeous private brain. That promise, that person I knew eons ago. *After surgery I think it'd be nice to try and have a baby with you.*

Ah, the dated stone worlds in my dented head, no assembly required, her carnation flesh held like a German church's stained glass in grout and granite, and my black wool holding me like blood in dirt. This ratty black sweater was a gift from her in NYC. Now her appealing apparition appearing to this apparatchik. Or perhaps here on the other side of the world it is reversed like the clocks and I am the apparition. Perhaps the woman by the hedge is alive and I am the dead one.

Peacocks caterwaul behind the carriage house and way down in the kelly-green depths of the ravine desperate salmon inch upstream, eyes jammed in the sides of their heads like green buttons, salmon crawling their gravel kitchen floor and launching themselves up turbine rapids like quivering rockets, coming back where they've been while seagulls bend to peck out their eyes.

On charnel banks we watch the salmon suffer in sequence. A path down through the birch and wild sunflowers to the water's edge and gravel bars – a spectator sport of sorts where we observe pure need. It seems I am always a spectator.

In Oregon once we went down to see the fish spawn.
We were recording in Portland, I think in that Kill Rock Stars studio.
She loves to speak Spanish, loves deserts, loves water.

Se puede nada aqui?
In Oregon so much love and then a tiny morsel of hate, a start.
May one swim here?

Si, pero tenga cuidado. Be careful. Watch out for rock stars. Ha.
Sometimes we were too careful. In Oregon she climbed into the river.

The river flows easily to the sea that waits. A lit world to the west of us, golden palisades cracking into rectangular blocks. Behind the church, quiet white horses stand in the meadow wind. It is late summer, or it's autumn's beautiful desolation, raw sienna, autumn's lingering decision, wood-smoke weather.

In the veiled garden where I stand, evening bats gamble as to how close they can flicker by my skull, my bats swoop sideways like hideous minor deities, a rush for them and a rush for me, a game, perhaps even mutual fun. *Company's coming*! Certainly I admire the ugly little bats, enjoy their unpredictable companionship, how they turn from a wall.

I hope you're happy, she wrote.

I will call Tuesday, she promised, *I will try to call.*

Why didn't she say, It's very likely I will *not* call Tuesday.

More soon, she emails, but there is never more.

But that's not fair. I used to not call in an earlier era. I still email *more soon*. My glancing callousness during low-throated phone calls, in cars and doors, the dizzy compass needle late at night. And now, on another continent, our backyard stance, our strange spaceship alertness, looking at each other, straw hair in her serious narrow eyes.

I love her eyes, our eyes are everything, but would it be a smoother world, smoother if not a single person could *see* another? If we had everything else, every other part, if we bumped and bumbled about as we do, but there was no such thing as a singular face to haunt you later? The eyes have it. She halts, her body facing the hedge, but her stony Roman-statue eyes turned toward me.

OUR SEVERE ALLEGIANCE during that time together, every swift minute bent to a single sinful republic. Our devotion there, alive, then fading into puzzling memories, frayed posters on power poles, last year's top ten hit.

On the road with the band I tend to revisit familiar locales: there's the kip pub that kicked me out three years ago. There's where I rented the bicycle with no gears. There's where we dropped the four-hundred-pound Hammond organ in the roadway.

In this way I'm a bit like the bloodied salmon in the ravine, retracing lost steps, losing their eyes to the beaks. But what is the attraction – why the drive away and the drive back home? I don't know, but I know I do it over and over. I have no home. How I miss this person, but she has been absent years now.

I got your letter and I love it! It made me laugh and feel lots of surges. Sorry I didn't call last night.

Can she still be a real person after all this maudlin mental abrasion we forced ourselves through after the split? Is she still someone real, or is she reduced to rich exhalations buried deep within brain cells, oxygen images shipwrecked in my stupid head? The word *crush*. Two thieves, we loved each other and we robbed each other of happiness. I have moments of joy; I can't always keep them in the best order, can't preserve them in amber or tar. Maybe that's all right. I'm not sure yet. In Euro-land I've been mainlining regret, really leaning into it. I will take it in every morning like a vinegar cereal. I will fondle its colours until regret becomes something positive and fierce. I am exquisitely drunk, as is most of the band.

In the lit mansion they are throwing dice on glowing pine and reading the drummer's mother's John O'Hara paperbacks. We are supposed to be recording the fabled follow-up album. But, where they hear Moog I hear banjo, *For the Turnstiles,* a song she liked.

Banjo? the band asks. *Are you out of your fucking mind?*

Maybe I am. I hear trombone on one new cut, I want ancient Ludwigs, a wrench jammed in the piano strings. On that minor key tune I want to play a C harp and get that Dorian thing happening. Maybe I'm losing the Czech techno influence, the Praha jungle feel, maybe we're going serious shoegazer, diving deeper into trance with a Kraftwerk *Lost in Space* vibe. Or the band is imploding.

And I'm having trouble coming up with even half-ass lyrics. Eyes, prize? Lips, ships? Maybe baby. So many faders at our fingers, too many choices: red buttons, green buttons, 64-track anxiety, that fear and paralysis at the board — what if I wreck it choosing the wrong way?

It sounds good with distortion. *No, no, it sounds good clean.*
Bring the vocals up. *No, bury the vocals more.*
Telecaster or clavinet? *Why are we always doing your songs?*

I miss the days of my old 4-track cassette in the bedroom. Now the band is produced, but we have produced no *product*. Too many fucking samples and egos and wired and tired arguments about instruments and songs and who the hell wrecked the vintage RCA ribbon mic.

Pan left track two, pan right track four, pan to the next room's attractive clink of exotic bottles and amazing loneliness of naked bodies.

When a child I wondered why the Beatles broke up. Now, in a band, I wonder how the Beatles lasted so long. Maybe we should journey to India and find a guru and pluck giant sitars.

A question, oh groovy guru living in my stupid head: she wears a dress; have I ever even seen her in a *dress*? Maybe it's a frock or a nightshirt lifting in a breeze. By the dark hedge she is about to move, though I can't move. The woman at the hedge is looking at me in a way I just cannot interpret at all. Bees, knees?

At the backdoor bees crawl over red paving bricks. No one else in the band has noticed, but on the cellar floor I keep finding dead bees. How are bees entering the lapstrake walls and stone cellar? Where is our lush queen? You levitate to a hundred flowers and you come hither to die in a basement. They come to me, they crawl at my bare feet; our house is now their hive; I feel connected, living in their hive.

Do the bees want to explain something to the band, confess something desperate to me before expiring? Or do the bees hope we will be pierced, step on last upturned stingers? This idea seems doubtful. But now I rule out nothing.

My aunt in North London walking down the stairs to calmly inform her husband, *I've been stung.*

A death sentence for her there among the oil paintings and giant oaks and horse paths and private schools. Stung. She knew she was supposed to get the pipette right away, a choice, but instead she tiptoed down to her husband in his sweater, disbelief and puzzlement in her last words. Her choice meant everything. She wanted to let him know, she desired to see him once more.

WHAT IS SHE saying under the hedge and northern lights, what words are those on her lips? Everything seems a surprise to me these days, these northern nights: *I didn't know that could happen to me. Or that.* That hurt. She is blond, but she reminds me of a young Elizabeth Taylor, her head, her mouth, night sky our big movie screen, bees on the bricks, moonlight on her neck, that cute little push-up affair, her necklace in my fingers' grasp; this all seems momentous and fragile to me.

What is it about flesh revealed to your eyes, to your fingers, the absolute power flesh possesses? Her dress seems out of focus, yet I can see that her fluted glass has bubbles trapped in clear liquid. I seem to be trapped with her, but she is not trapped with me. That's hardly cricket.

Maybe the band should have gone to Jamaica to record. My wallet must be around here somewhere. I doubt if we'll make our dates down in Australia. Is it summer down under or warm winter?

Times we travel and I feel like a chimpanzee locked in some tin can space capsule, invisible lab-coat parties feeding data and codes and liquids, steering my collection of retro rivets and fried dials through orbits and stars and stellar way stations, and satellites running stop signs in outer space (*hey asshole, learn to fucking drive*), my brake lights sparking in time's eternal milk darkness, our universe lit by spilt milk and the inefficient engine of mixed feelings. I play bass and keys. I am the way.

THE APOSTLE DOUBTING THOMAS wanted to finger Christ's wounds before he would believe anyone big comes back to bozos like us. Dylan Thomas, all bee-stung lips and Welsh accent, set some kind of eejit whisky record at the White Horse Tavern. I can't be satisfied, I'm a king bee, buzzing round your hive, I want to come inside. *Honeycomb, won't you be my baby*. At the hedge she looks at me as if studying foggy X-rays and coming to the inevitable conclusion, a Henry Kissinger exit strategy. She does not move, but I know an exit is pending, an exit wound, her predicated words waiting like a Smiths B-side.

The flight was delayed again, a bent cargo door. Maybe someone punched it. Feels like I haven't talked to you in ages, though it's only a day; maybe that's too long. I can't wait to see you, laugh with you in person.

ALL THE LUGGAGE held and runways extended just for us. We flew over that stunning Iron Age beach; we tried to surf freezing growlers, but I kept falling on my face in the water and she couldn't stop shaking. Cold wintergreen water filling her top and dragging her shorts down past her white hips and she had goosebumps everywhere.

"It's not too bad," she said with chattering teeth, a crown of Irish cliffs leaning hugely behind her face, "not too bad once you're in."

I didn't care then, but now want to be in her.

She tried to please, a peacemaker when I was volatile, stupid in the village pub. For a few centuries the ocean pushes sand one way, while wind from the land pushes seeds and dunes the other way. Everyone has a turn, has a go at it.

Tides and winds meet and braid something gorgeous, forge this glorious beach with sandy dunes and soft hills sliding behind its length; Vikings laid eyes on this conflicted shore. Forces meet head-on and alter the misty landscape, but eventually they separate, lose each other.

I will begin again, forget her again, commence the canyon erosion in my head all over once more, that stupid necessary erosion, forty thousand headmen, the river flows, it flows to the sea, out damn spot, wind and dirt scraping, lake blowing salt, rivers running in silt and salt and rubbery salmon eggs.

Love migrates like sand in surf, ink migrates, raffish rat-face sharks keep moving in surges and yolk-coloured breakers and briny undersea clouds. Sharks and jets move on paths, contrails, where their noses take them. What did your luggage look like? No nostalgia allowed, please just confine yourself to dealing with reality.

My private theory on matters of the heart, despite the opinion of well-paid therapists and my well-intentioned sister, is to *not* stir up sediment; my theory is to leave it all alone. Cowboy up, get back on that horse, run through the jungle. I get in a state and what can I say, *L'etat c'est moi.*

THIS LIT WOODEN MANSION fills with dying bees and I have told almost every person in this small nation state to fuck off; perhaps it is time to move on, to be rid of certain honey-combed brain cells and arc-welding visions, time to destroy this homestead, like artillery penetrating oak trunks.

Love is hardly blind, but sometimes we need glasses, correctives, dogs and bells, ropes and belts, hawsers and harnesses, better song lyrics. No hard feelings, one hopes. We were good for each other.

To canoe her to a leafy island, a hidden grove of sunny butternut trees, a soft red blanket. My dislike of condoms. *O careless love*! Once her eyes closed in a brick house, hair down in those eyes, and her iron-black headboard and patchwork quilt and her second thoughts, her "understandable concerns" about me: was I clean, was I fooling around, would she catch something from me, was there a dark future of caveats and the tingle of cold sores? But our past! Our past is without footnotes or flaws. Our past has such shiny teeth.

AS CHILDREN WE walk in naïve riotous parades and mobs, foot soldiers in our temporary empires. As giant-headed children we plucked the hedge's tiny honeysuckle blossoms and tore the tiny blossoms apart to mouth the sweetness hidden inside our parents' garden.

We aimed our white telescopes at the sputnik heavens, so much room up there, more room as each opportunity escapes.

The new cherries broke open in the hot interior valley, broke in sudden pure rain, and Bill the orchard owner's crop was ruined.

This reversal, this negation of life. The big question: What did I give up and what did I gain?

One night in a new town it hit me; I stepped down blond pine stairs in windowed moonlight and felt like my aunt in London stung by a bee: I was plainly still here in flesh and blood and light from a planet's giant humming sky, but I felt numbered amongst the walking dead. I had known two amazing worlds and one had just been yanked from my fingers. I felt exiled, envious of those I knew still drinking and playing acoustic guitars on the roof of the ratty rented house (*can you please crawl out your window*). These people seemed so important, even when they are not important and may be toxic and may be fools.

Later you may find a new life that is superior in its fresh oxygen. But that in-between time must somehow be endured.

Who now will sleep with whom in the neglected orchard, laughing over their Irish whiskey and skullcap mushrooms and Dilaudid. Who will break the Decemberists' mandolin? Who will leverage a broad city avenue into the smallest vein? It's all the rage. No money in their pants, yet they buy booze, cigs, word of mouth CDS, nights out, nights in — always night, and her mouth closing on me. All my rage. A mouth can occlude, include, slake, take.

Just in from the dentist — mouth frozen, a feeling I hate. But I love you, would like to kiss your nice mouth. I think I was flat and a bit distant during our talk Tuesday. My head was bad, I was feeling drugged, everything on a kind of delay.

KEYBOARDS RAMP UP in the big house, someone on my old analog fooling around on "Green Onions." Musical notes moving into the outside air, and then she moves. Eyes still meeting mine, she slips into the huge verdant hedge that curves out like the side of a giant body, the hedge that rises over us like ribs. Walls of dark green, a hedge so green it's almost black. Her loose dress glowing like cataract marble, but she vanishes. She moves into the giant body's side as silently and easily as a steak knife, she enters the body and the body doesn't notice until later.

Check one-two!

Delmore the wing-nut drummer kicks away the metronome and click track, Delmore's drums and high hat tripling the tempo, Klaus's Roland keyboard driving minor key unease, pushing out fat sound like custard over a scratch guitar that dwells like a devil in dub reverb.

She has vanished into the hedge and ripeness is all. There is an opening in the twilight, as if for a ghost, a gap open in blue-green air. She is gone. You can put your fingers in the wounds — you can slide through like a quarter into a slot machine and there you are on the other side of the hedge.

The drummer kicks away, and my theremin and custom teak bass and rolling tapes await me, but I can't seem to shift from my lovely spot in the marred starry garden, from my cloudland ceiling, my mottled universe of surf. Nothing is ever really dead. Where else to go but backwards? It's all the rage. What other direction is there?

This week was brutal, locked out of the car once and locked out of the house twice. Last night there was talk of your flirting ways. I'm jinxed. Feels like I haven't chatted with you in ages. Wish we could be strolling by the river. Listening to "Sad-Eyed Lady of the Lowlands." *I can't wait to see you. Will I see you?*

TWO AMAZING PLANETS and life on both — this is not something you can verify easily or scientifically. Dear Sir or Madam: Even though you are connected by payphones likes two tin cans with string, we regret to inform you that you can't know that other life burning like a porthole, a grease fire, you can't know that jolly corner, that shady lane, that vain dreamlife you might have known in her cedar attic, on distant discounted moons or stars or unmoored streets or that unmade bed on the far side of your verdant childhood hedge.

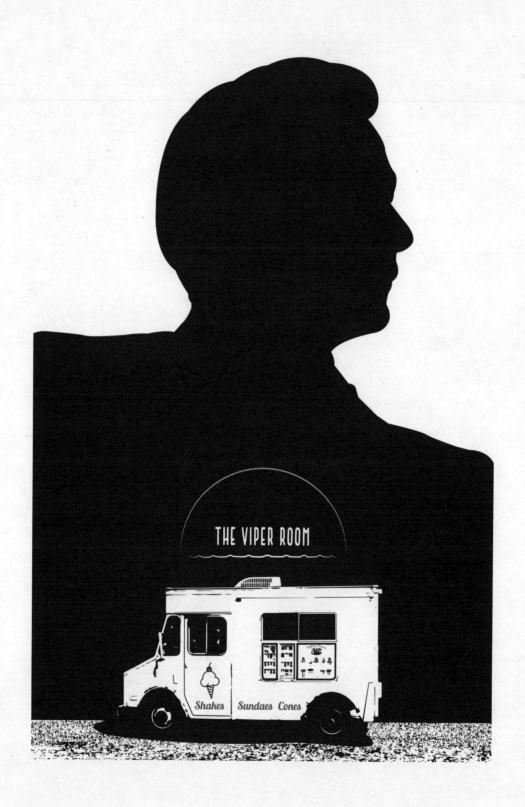

JOHNNY CASH IN THE VIPER ROOM (COWBOY ASYLUM)

For centuries I waited inside, waited out those fierce Irish immigrants on their black Blasket rocks surrounded by waves and weird red-legged birds and Viking raiders on the horizon. I was inside them, a salty cell or two, like a tiny starfish glued to a rock, and now I am risen in southern California, rising at dawn with a longboard to scan the surf breaks and weak peelers and some hours later I drive crowded miles on Route 1 to enlighten you re: today's inevitably disappointing specials.

"My name is Michael and I'll be your server," I say, practising my new lines while bent like some hunchback, arachnid, almost on all fours surfing the rabid curl. "Do you have reservations?"

Fall into surf and the ocean eats me, but the drowned rat look is huge here. "I want us to keep in touch," Anna said once. Sure, okay, that seems nice. I felt stupid, but later I followed her down, that north to south routine, the bottom of Canada to the top of Mexico. I have reservations, I think to myself. Many reservations.

ANNA AND I HAVE A HISTORY, we walked the waxed halls of the same windowless school, we skied hazy Chinese-looking mountains together, Goat's Eye, Devil's Chimney, rolling numbers on the chairlift to a peak, ascending, both of us descended and decoded from those dramatic Blasketmen who got loaded on illegal batches of *poteen*, island families rarely even making it from the Blaskets onto the Irish mainland.

Of course high school sweethearts are doomed. Anna likes the *idea* of California, orange groves in the valley, the pier at Santa Monica, X and the Blasters playing Madame Wong's club, no weather. Anna adores Rivers Phoenix or Phoenix Rivers or whatever his name is, has a big poster of him looking sensitive on her wall.

"Something about him seems okay," she says, "really real, not like those phoney stars." She wrote an essay about him for school, is a bit of a fan. But then he's in the Viper Club washroom, a snort of Persian Brown. "This'll make you feel fabulous." His universe wrenched in a moment.

Those rangy-tang islanders, on the Blaskets, they were just different, separated by storms, weather, separated by DNA and Blasket Sound's four miles of treacherous water, separated by generations from that life and they didn't care a fig. There is something different about islands. Algerian pirates landed there in the 1600s and stole flitches of bacon and stole women for slaves, harems in the Mediterranean. I pity those poor women snatched from their garden, running barefoot and nowhere to run, *their* universe wrenched in a moment: what kind of brutal life were those women dragged to? The orange sails by the island, a ship sailing away, the women below with the sailors. I've stepped on that island beach, the black cliffs and the tricky paths down to the rolling breakers, the Atlantic.

"Thank you," I sputter as I surf, as I wipe out in the drink, the Pacific, nostrils full of saltwater. "Sit wherever you like."

I don't belong here in California or at this upscale lobster palace, but Anna left me in Montana, she came down here tempted by, you know, the standard list: decent burritos, the promise of deco laundromats, the twenty-three-year-old star in OD mode.

"I can't breathe," the star tells his sister Rain. "Take me outside," he says, then thrashing his fine, famous head on the sidewalk for several minutes outside Johnny Depp's club on Sunset Strip. That high grade Persian Brown or China White or Crystal Meth or Yukon Mindfuck, *fabulous*, and now the shrine to his death takes up the sidewalk. The Valium didn't help him, he was on his own outside the Viper Room.

How many in your party? Who knows. Always a third walking with us.

Who are your people? the charming older people ask me. Our ancestors and uncles believed themselves lordly – now this is going way back – believed themselves separate from the Irish, our own island kingdoms of collision and kinships, our curraghs made of hides, such tiny boats in high waves and maritime noise and pointed kingdoms of stone, my ancestors boasting bright red sashes, black hats with flat brims, their clothes almost Spanish, flamboyant, dancers on stone and heather, and their feet danced as if always perched on a narrow boat, in their muscles, like surfing, learning tiny movements and corrections, directions home, human gyroscopes, in curraghs like dark kayaks spinning out after a few fish, a load of peat, the smell of both cargoes a given, something genetic, in you like algebra, like endorphins.

Balance comes to you, bodies come to you. Bodies nimble up high on a narrow boat, but not so nimble down in the wide water. No one can swim, no one learns that. Canada is due west of the Blaskets; Newfoundland's trash floats there.

On their stone island, brown rabbits gallop high windy paths on the cliffs and three hills, thousands of birds but no trees, no wood anywhere, imagine that, burning turf hauled from the mainland, sheep and peat piled in tiny boats, surf surging up and down greasy rocks, shore the worst spot, bodies stuck in white surf, pinned, though moving up and down, and a young woman like Anna wondering whose young brother is that drowning? The surf eats you. Up and down, familiar bodies, familiar backs, face down, so close, gannets smashing water and magically out again, but drowned brothers don't come out again and mourners on a black cliff stare down from tiny paths beaten in grass, less and less of them left on the island, and then the grandparents shipped the hell off by the government and their island sold from under them like a used car.

ANNA MY EX is Viking blood, remnant of ancient raids, ancient rape, prow scraping the beachhead. Her form and favours, a pure product of those wars and attacks, and I can't get her out of my blood. At high school talent night we sang a duet of "Girl from the North Country," her doing the Dylan part, me attempting Johnny Cash.

Anna moved away, moved to Tacoma and Seattle and Calgary and Vancouver, went to college, waitressed, worked a record store in a Chinatown alley, came back home looking altered. Anna wants to travel, move on. Everyone moved on, emigrants scattered and I followed inside my people (*Who are your people?* they ask). Anna and I were possibilities, coals glowing, codes hidden in clouds of sperm, scattered, moving. Inside of those people (*my* people!), I vaguely drifted through those families and famines, lived inside my grandmothers and great uncles, hurlers and coopers, lived invisibly in the DNA of demented second cousins who fought the Boers, the Huns, fought the big one, went through depression and the Depression, *made it run on time*. Our Canadian uncles landed puking and shooting at Dieppe and likely some other branch of Holy Roman Empire relatives shot back at them.

We were all so cold in the surf, went through the Cold War, Anna and me, shivering, goosebumps, order goose-down parkas from Land's End.

THE FAMOUSLY FATUOUS, famously crooked Irish politician owns one of the Blasket Islands now, owns an island and a yacht and stud horses on a civil servant's salary. Stunning views of the Atlantic and

Dingle Bay and Kerry's mountains and to the south the Skellig rocks rising like glass pyramids out of the sea. The pretty lines of surf where we survived Viking raiders in the tenth century, survived the English, the Dutch, Spanish, Algerians, the priests, but the islanders can't stand up to the twentieth century.

IN 1853 OR 55 my great-grandfather sailed to America, a man following a woman the way I follow Anna from Canada. Tralee, Liverpool, Boston's docks and the Quincy market, but they lay nauseous on separate ships. Was he too late? He followed new rails west, *clickety-clack*, and each tie laid on the ground a dead Irishman, a man killed working the railroad. Later I worked for the railroad, but the job got cut. My great-grandfather walked his way across a new country: the bricks of Chicago, the Minnesota Massacre, south to Show-Me Missouri and Kansas City, joining the US army, cavalry, deserting the army as soon as he got out west to go mining, wandering way north to Powder River and Crow's Nest and Butte, the mines down deep, big sky at the top of a hole, copper, silver, dynamite, fire in the hole, shafts flooding and my genes moving through good brick bars, narrow and long and dark, long godless brawls wrecking Victorian bars, oak furniture and fixtures, all that hard work and hard alcohol and devoted orgiastic destruction.

One hundred years later, Anna and I touch our fingers, touch coins on those same giant mahogany bars, ornately carved and chiselled and dragged up the Mississippi and overland to tiny railroad and cattle towns that were booming, but now quietly evaporating.

In my dad's air-conditioned Buick LeSabre I drive to them, I will follow, an explorer, an ambulance chaser. Oh gold-rush hotel, Oh milky flyspeck windows, Oh Bitterroot Mountains! I will study bloodshot maps and eat Fred Radomski's deer sausage and drink warm bottles of beer at the ornate bar with Anna in white pants and her glassy eyes always looking beyond me, far out the windows made buttery by a century of smoke. My great-grandfather didn't find her, he was too late.

These lost American towns just under Canada's shadow have a wall-eyed, one-sided look: towns facing train yards and stockyards that are vanished, vast railroad hump-yards and cow-calf schools of protein and glue and lumberyards, facing what is no longer there for the eye, though you sense all of it. The closed store, the bankrupt implement dealer, lopsided towns out of balance, like gandy dancers poised on a railroad track, like ghostly Blasketmen about to exit a rocking boat.

Dilaudid, Oxy, E, Special K, BC home-grown, Rolling Rock, Coors, gin, Crown Royal. For a while Anna and I used the border for personal gain, crossing lines, moving choice items in different directions — pills, whisky, movies, coin-op TVs, Xboxes — nothing serious or hard, avoiding the bigger crossings, the cameras — money to be made on both sides of the line, driving up to the Badlands, the Blood reserve, lost riverbank coal mines and dinosaur bones, way up there past the Going-To-The-Sun Road, which seems the roof of the world, though it is not the roof of the world. Canada is above, a river over a river, another world on top of a world.

ANNA KNOWS HER WAY through yellow hills and controlled burns, a good driver, used to gravel and distance. She knows back ways and ways back; she plunges us through gaps in the map, gaps the glacier left. More room for bottles and TVs and video games and Ziplocs with the backseat pulled out of her sedan. Rolling down from quiet Canada we listen to Skip James, Wall of Voodoo, haunted muzak and Anna stops the car in her meadow of glacial erratics, big grey boulders the buffalo used to scratch their itch, and me itching, mosquitoes into me, me into her, bonfires and bottles, blankets that won't stay put, stars over pines, lunar coteaus, grape-coloured mountains, tilted mountains with alternating stripes like some crushing parfait, white snow and black shale, miles of river breaks, ashen soil and wheat, landscape rippled, wrinkled like Anna's fine brain, wrinkled like her loose flannel shirt minus a button or two and I am lord of the trembling hand.

ANNA'S FIVE BROTHERS raise gazehounds, sleek retrievers, and whippets: low noses permanently to the ground, seriously insane cattle dogs. The dogs play games with coyotes, but the five brothers shoot any coyote dead as a nit, lost too many calves to coyotes; the coyotes isolate the calves in the skinny poplars and pin them down in their own rain of blood.

Rain falls on Anna in the back of the pickup, in the yard by the gas tank on stilts, lightning and hard rain leaking into the mudroom at the back door, rain drifting from the dedicated purple storm, the storm with its TV-related duties and numbers. The brothers all tall, a sect of ball-cap clones with dark hair and I cannot tell them apart.

"You hungry?" The ball-cap brothers shoot their way through life, shoot their way through tiny birds to cook tiny dishes, the creatures fly into the scalding iron pan, miniature guts into the fire. They fry a snake or two, drive the snakes from their land, drive out the buffalo, build fences, mend walls, open the doors, and Anna's drinking in the bar with her brothers, Butte, Montana crazy on St. Patrick's Day, lunatic drunks fighting, heads smashing brick, bloody walls and fancy bluegrass falsettos from arched gothic jukeboxes that belong in a cathedral.

Anna waits in the M&M Cigar Store looking angry and private. Because of her ways, I now view angry and private women in a different light: they seem possible and compelling where others see a write-off only. Now that Anna is gone, I study serious women and wonder, don't I know them a bit.

"Lo there, Charlie," I say to the grizzled bartender.

A drunk man stands at the bar, yells, "Oh yeah, swerve on there, buddy!" He has giant feet like a clown, he buys me a Mexican beer and I return the favour.

Anna possesses a Don't Mess With Me public face, but we have our moments of fun – had our moments. I felt I already knew her face when I met her, or else I knew her well in several slow moments, knowing the same sturdy limbs my great uncles knew and followed, fell for, the fringe of hair over her private eyes. I don't like a car right on my ass. I'm not a leader – I'm happy to follow, let them get the ticket.

Anna's demeanour relaxed me somehow, there was no acting when we were alone, unless that itself is an act. I'm not really sure now, and of course time plays tricks, a brain plays tricks on its own brain, goes back in time to make little adjustments, and a brain goes forward too, onward, upward — move close to her at all and brain and a lower organ responds as if by instinct, knowledge, blood forward, an immigrant in a new land translating the selfish landlord's missive. Look at my diction, my interests. How my dear ancestors would despise me.

THERE ARE GANGS of Irish here in our high-plain boondocks, but they do not count, they are common, from every county in Eire, but they are not Blasket Islanders. A drummer the height of a leprechaun leads a string band at the crossroads dance. What is this place we find as we drive? It's like the extreme west of Ireland, I see my ancestor's stovepipe hats still around, smoking clay pipes like my great-uncles, our own eyebrows and faces surround us.

Chinooks, mud, killer dust, snow then mud again. These plains held under the mountains are a long way from sharp islands and Spanish faces and eyebrows, the shawled mourners, the black Irish of rumour, of olive skin and dark brows, of Spanish shipwrecks and sailors, luckless or tricked onto rocks by lights for salvage, for treasure. Those Irish shipwreck tales are likely a load of shite, but perhaps a kernel of truth there. Some of the locals do look the part and Spain is not far as the crow flies or the sailing smack steers.

I'm in the car's passenger seat. They stare at me and the serious woman driving.

"How you making out," I ask the stovepipe hat people.

"Copacetic, I suppose," they reply.

Doesn't Anna yell, "Help! Help! He's kidnapped me! Help! Oh take pity on poor me if you're any kind of men!"

What the hell is Anna doing? Then Anna hits the gas and speeds away.

"Why the hell'd you do that?" I ask.

"What? Lighten up," Anna says. "It was funny."

"Lighten up? Bags of pharmaceuticals and you yell, *He kidnapped me*." I keep looking in the rear-view for State Troopers, but maybe they're off quelling riots on the state farm or fighting wars in the Middle East. "I was about to ask if they were Irish, if they were my people. I wanted to know."

"Oh, you wanted to know," Anna says. "Maybe some other time, huh. We'll come back some other time, bucko," she says flatly.

What do you make of that? Like it's a company picnic that got rained out.

AFTER WW II ANNA's family hit oil and had leases and flare-offs and her family went to hell in a classic manner: big fins on the car, trips to Hawaii in the winter, her father's cigar and glittering eyes, huge loans against the land, buying up more and more quarter sections and sections until the farm shows up on satellite maps, rivals the Hutterite spreads. Then the downturn, the recession, the new marching orders from a distant head office, the phone calls to the kitchens from local bank managers, and Anna's father's suicide.

"Got to talk to you pronto," says the banker. "This is not up to me," he explains.

Low prices, high interest, can't make the durn deal work no how. Sell off chunks of land and sell some more, no more trips to the dentist, stop painting the red buildings. One of the lanky brothers beat up the banker after he called in their loans, beat the man badly, pulled a little jail time (inside joining the Aryan Nation boys and once out of the Deer prison he moved west to the mountain valleys of Idaho). Rip open the mail, the money gone, collateral gone, negative figures on the monthly statements.

Some are killed by war, earthquakes; some of us are killed by fine print, small details. Walk away from the ranch, the woman, the island, sold out, pushed off our little islands. Anna's father won't walk, won't talk, the burly widower lights a final cigar, shoots his dogs, then shoots himself. Coyotes sit across the highway, watching the man's swayback barn burning like a painting, a Carl Beam acrylic.

AND I'M AFRAID Anna will burn her house down with her candles everywhere, her antique bed and available light, candles hung in pewter storm lanterns, light the colour of an anvil. Anna is not clumsy, has grace on her feet, but such is her luck that her room could burn and I worry about her and always will. In California she tells me she is couch surfing. On the phone I am suspicious, sick, envisioning different tanned men on her, tattooed miscreants, mutant beach-boys, indie metalhead drummers. That's so *fascinating*, she would think of some malnourished dork, how *edgy*.

Yes, if by edgy you mean moronic and a lifetime of bad decisions.

Couch surfing, bah. I remember her green family couch and our happy hours sailing on it. Nice just to lean on each other. A shirt coming off, leaning over her like a cliff and a beach, nature breathed on us, nature hated us, put us together.

I remember each of Anna's ribs, the fingers progress up, each to each (in Canada I was the only one on the road), hand reaching under Anna's legs from behind and asking, *Who are your people?* while readying the long English for business. We are all breathing, we are works-in-progress.

But, dear reader, my plump partridge drinks, my vixen is moody. Things seemed not bad, but Anna had some lifestyle questions. Then several local bikers explain they don't appreciate us selling our wares on their turf, politely asking us to cease and desist. The full-patch bikers, they are good with language, they're moving dump trucks of coke, they have little machines that count money and they must keep their various machines humming.

Before going south, Anna spoke to me of new horizons, journeys to self-esteem, validation, closure, me doing the goddam dishes once in a blue moon. If there was a message I didn't really care to listen. There are times it is better not to know.

One day Anna gives away her books and plants and fishing rods, cancels cable and drives a used ice cream truck through Utah to LA, water pump shrieking in protest, sliding doors open and cold air off the mountains rushing through the back of the ice cream van. She's gone, Daddy, gone.

MONTHS LATER, MOMENTS LATER I followed her down (*baby won't you follow me down*). I drove a car up the Grapevine like it was a waterfall, I was wounded, I wondered and wandered fallen basins of Los Angeles. The mountains at the avenue's end, driveways everywhere, red tiled roofs, signs in Spanish, and I squandered time working as a dough fry man, rent-a-cop, valet, framer. Park that car! Stow that trash! Clean the terrazzo! Whip those weeds, tote that barge! Wait for the clock hands and watch for the fingers peeling cash off a roll. It's better than a *maquiladaro*.

The driver with yellow beacons and plainly worded signs about the immediate future, that little car that warns us that a big trailer or wide load is imminent – that's a job I could handle. Hear ye hear ye, Paul Revere here, **WIDE LOAD** coming down the pike. Late at night pedal steel sounds sublime, I'd pay someone to play pedal steel as I go to sleep, as I still cannot find her in California's rolling brownouts.

Cal Edison and Pacific Gas & Electric are insolvent, no windmills running, no gas turbines, the new humility and hostility. Blackouts in Santa Monica for lunch and Sunset Boulevard blacked out for supper. In California's dimming lights I will find her. They give out mandatory sunglasses at the state line; if she's wearing sunglasses in the blackout, I will do the same. The ocean shoulders right up against the Mexican border; I expect a dayglo yellow stripe across the water.

Little turnstiles mark the Mexican border, as if a country is a soccer stadium. Canada does not exist down here. Canada's borders have a church-like hush, the air incensed with ritual and guilt, confession and relief. This southern portal is carnival, revelry, hurly-burly. Down at the southern docks boats bump, Mexican men in outfits not that far removed from my family several generations before, and I am reminded not of cheese-head Canada, but of Ireland, men in hats, women in bright shawls, lost islands, lost uncles, every mother's son. There are even horse races on the strand, post to post, exiles from Iberia, Hibernia, and modern kayaks the exact size of my ancestors' boats made of hide and tar.

You can balance, you can dance across boats, each a fibreglass shoe, can cover miles down to a border walking on the water. I'm confused; I can't tell if this world is old or new, Spanish or WASP. In Tijuana I see Johnny Cash drinking Bohemia and Negra Modelo with his daughter Rosanne and Rodney Crowell looking neither happy nor unhappy. He has evaded the Viper Room. As if waiting to cross, they sit by the river, but there are no seats near them.

Years before I drove up to Canada to see Johnny Cash sing in a hockey barn, a picture of the Queen above his pomade head. She seemed to disapprove. His record label had dropped him, he was playing small towns and the faithful gathered there. Guitar pointing, he charged around the small stage like a rhino. I don't know if he was past the pills yet. Now he sits by the river looking older than that hockey arena night, deep grooves in his face, jowls, wispy grey hair. He has travelled from 1950s greaser to Old Testament prophet.

Dogs wander ravines in Mexico and I step into yet another new life, head altered like a carrot by a shovel, step into a bar and drink mescal instead of *poteen*, exchange worlds, our talents carried within like gin in a gut, like lost connections, strange voices on water bumping like boats, islands pointed. You can't balance, can't stay, just a minute in her, salvage and salvation, our hidden slippery harbours, hulls so close

[41]

to the rocks, what we treasure so close, we crash or we deliver the goods, push into harbour, insert slot A into flap B.

In a crowd of tattoos and goatees I walk back to San Diego, cross the border, our DNA with us, beauty and beast-ugly both, our DNA working the room.

Anna goes into her new place with her DNA, her wet swimsuit, and I follow. Anna gives me her new number. I found her at the shrine to the dead star, I see her now against a pink wall. "I've lost weight," she says. "I'm down to 110."

Anna is changing. I know her skin is white and cold under the wet bathing suit, now Anna is changing into a long light hippie dress in the sun, I know this item from Montana. Now she has a poster of Depp looking sensitive; she's moved on. Anna wrecks her ankle on the stairs, why is she so clumsy? Wrong decisions, me one of them. Me and my current lack of relation with the lines of her familiar thin underwear. A line of panties like sailboat pennants on her shower curtain, but none for me. I can't see, but I know from experience that, as Anna leans forward to talk, I know that one elastic borderline across her backside dips lower and reveals more, and an almost vertical line swoops down, curving down under her, another border, but here I can't cross.

I look in her eyes and talk, drink red tea, slice apples with her dead uncle's bone knife, her section and my section. I bring her that special pungent cheese she loves. I look in her wary eyes, my blood telling me to just walk to her, cross state lines into her, to follow yet again, an immigrant with no brains. Who cares about her new movie star boyfriend.

California silicon breasts up everywhere. Anna says, "I had a kid young so I never had a chance to be perky." My ex-girlfriend who drops tears and shakes her fist at God. Mexican kids sell gum at the busy border. Her kid gone, it was when she was away, her private sorrow, Anna doesn't like to talk at times. We are disconnected.

"I do want us to stay in touch," she says. "I'm just not good at it," she adds as a codicil.

Back in Montana Anna was sleeping under sheets, a diorama. *Wake up, wake up,* I whispered, *hurry*. I just have a minute or two then I have to go, passing by, wanted to say hi. My bread truck around the corner, I opened the door, came up the stairs, she's warm, her ass covered up and her soft breasts uncovered, my mouth hadn't been on Anna in so long, forgotten her taste, *wake up*, I say, she's sleepy, *hurry*, just a minute, fast, like violent air around a train, then we go back to being ordinary, the parade stops. That was the last time, baby the last time.

Now we come from separate islands, islands moving apart. She is another person. I go surfing at dawn, a surfer, your server, a serf. Those women stolen from the Blasket Islands by Algerian pirates — where are their offspring? Do their children walk southern shores and curse The Great Satan? All these eons of history, all this trading and scrounging and brawling at Fair Day and fires and crops and black-faced sheep and wonderful light sprawling on water, all these generations and genetics I seem to know or remember, all this leading down to this lobster shack and a star's skull banging the pavement from too much junk taken in. River had a blue coffin. Maybe I can meet his sister Rain, sing a duet with Rain.

How long have I lived in California now? I can barely remember. In California there is no such thing as memory. I love my new accountant, my new accent, my new place where light pushes over everything like a table of pastries and punchbowls at the hotel on the strip.

"Who stole my tips? Michael! Where is everyone!? Who's got table 5?!"

"No idea."

My father would insist, *When you're older you'll understand. Do you follow me, boy?* he'd ask. *Do you follow?*

Up in Canada there are wolves moving and wolf-willow shading a stream, and cool wind in a world's frenetic grasses. My empty childhood steppes. I follow, all right. Down here it's devil's weather, cars, narrow boats, pointed boats, young men drowning, too many surfers brawling in the crowded waves, and wary tourists won't step in the door.

In narcotic convulsions, a head bangs the sidewalk, Anna's hippie dress rattles on a metal hanger, a surfboard floats by itself. Bodies come to you. We study the water in dread, guessing at intent, to face some wave we can't know. Who are these aliens, who are these crazed pirates come to destroy us? Are they us? I have no idea, lost my Panavision, lost my sense of home on the range. We scan the horizon glare, that border, sense something out there past the power of our eyes. You entertain vague hopes that the referee will move you half the distance to the goal line, but instead Johnny Appleseed morphs into the meth lab in the desert.

PINE SLOPES, SWEET APPLE SLOPES

Joyful sleep, my snoring an adagio nocturne, but who is this demented accordion player wheezing on our street and waking me at dawn, what nimble swine is waking our long block of sleepers?

I was working the sawmill twelve straights hours, worked and then I drank too much Black Horse Porter in The Elephant Hotel, drank too much too late.

To cease the sun most mornings I would happily pay fifty dollars, just to once wake feeling sweet and fresh, but the clock conspires with alcohol and I seem to come to consciousness in guilt's astounding grey blanket, in grainy sheets like twists of prefabricated concrete and there I am set, there I am *curing*.

AND NOW THIS jeezly racket, oh who the hell is this crazy walker with a squeaky squeezebox, bellows peopled with malcontent mice.

It's not her redheaded husband, is it? Or is it the pale girl hit by lightning? A hangover lends me such fiercely attuned hearing and morality. Never again will I find sheepish sleep or my youthful tilt or that mystery shirt.

THIS DAWN ACCORDION bleats notes, yawns its song open, shuts a verse sharply, slurs and closes off odd chords, truncated, swallowed air. Then I hear Sally's broom move down a wooden porch like a subtle drummer using brushes, and *listen*, there is a contra yowl of cat's vocals, now a second cat in harmony, and *listen*, now a second broom!

Hush sir hush sir, go the brooms, and the tick tock mantel clock jumps in time. Morning dew drips from eaves into my rain barrel, *blip blip blip*, wooden doors creak open and creak shut on jittering Junebug avenues, doors open and shut in time to the cursed jaunty squeezebox, and who is thump thumping that carpet?

AT THE ELEPHANT HOTEL petty cash is kept in the oak and tin icebox and men in bowler hats and starched shirts are already shunting in for a quick shot at the gin-mill bar, cock-eyed men flapping gums, green Dutch door swinging, yellow bottles clunking on wood, wide jaws flapping and teeth clacking, avid palaver parsed at The Elephant, accelerando bartender muttering and moving quickly, picking up dead soldiers from bar or table top while Irish Molly sells dead partridges, partridges offered to gentlemen at fifty cents a dozen.

"Acey-deucey," sings Bill the balding card shark holding his arm high, "and a trey," smacking down his happy hand, a carved table leaping with coins of silver and gold.

Sweet Jesus I ask you, can't they *please* be silent a minute and let me try for a second sleep? But sleep is gone, sleep is royally screwed, sleep is following the strangling accordion down the road apiece, in the arms of Murphy et al. The whole street conspires, the street this morning an atonal arabesque band – doghouse howls, singing bells, the low rich sound of wagon traces' slap and tickle. It is no fecking use.

I give up, rise for a meal, something simple, a tin of sweetened milk, my spoon tinkling rough ceramic. Milk wavers into weak tea; that sparse second before they mix. Like river and sea, like meeting someone – those first moments with sweet Sally.

Or the girl in the field – that blood-white second before the lightning met her and hit only her.

INSIDE THE ELEPHANT HOTEL we open curved green bottles and reluctant clams and we open giant incensed territories: life seems easy, dangerous, violent, calm. We speak often of joy. There are no police or soldiers here to hinder our progress in the new world. New Denmark is not a prison; there is much cheap land past Mount Zion's heap of peeled pines and peeled spuds.

"GODDAMN TOLL ROADS, every few miles someone sticking out his fecking hand to collect a toll for his fecking section of mud road. Sick of it."

Men at my arm drink mead and porter dark as molasses, men drink Chain Lightning and strong Portland rum and Wenham Lake ice with little flakes of sawdust still on it.

"Can I buy a snatch of tobacco from ya?"

"You may."

When the hotel ran out of tobacco last winter we smoked short bits of dried roots in a scrap of newspaper.

YES, TO BE DEPRIVED makes you appreciate things. Sally dilutes the cask of Corpse Reviver that I found hidden in the dreamy cold lake and gave to her; she sells jam jars of this brown hooch or barters it for foodstuffs, a box of tea, an orange, incandescent beets, a suspiciously aged flitch of bacon.

"I'm half corned," says the freighter.

"Here's to the next half," offers a miner.

"I'll drink to that."

THAT WOMAN. HOW MUCH land there is in Sally's smoky eye, giant steppes, lost horizons, mapless miles. She says, "I fear no one but God and I fear him mightily." We are surrounded; here there is no escape from here.

I am too much in my own heated head; it's not healthy.

"I DRANK TOO MUCH," the blacksmith says to me at The Elephant Hotel, meaning, *I ache for that woman, but she does not ache for me; now what is the divine purpose of that? What is the science or biology or genetics behind that mix? How does that aid propagation of the species? A dead end, obviously, but why can't I pry her from my mind?*

I understand and I silently agree with every word he does not utter. Just to be close to a woman for even a minute I haul cold water from the spring, balance two porcelain containers. As you know, two are easier than one.

LIKE AN ELEPHANT, I remember sex, to be allowed once to dig into her map, the middle provinces, the middle parts of fortune, her bent at her wooden table and me working tenderly to open her, open her with two rough hands, good, good, she is wet, and that rich stew rises in my nostrils, primal, turn away from it a bit, she reaches under and grabs me, steers it, will it fit yet (*why then I'll fit ye*). We explore, adjust, push, we get going nimbly, and she becomes airborne. Fraught can be good and bad; this was good fraught. Very best.

AT THE WHITE CHURCH our raspy voices sing, *I'm working on a building*. And, weirdly, most of us *are* working on buildings! Birds flute above our ears and children sing a cappella in cloth caps while a dog pulls his little travois over a bagatelle clatter of clamshells.

Ah, all this noisome hooting noise, a world of noise (*hast thou clothed her neck with thunder*).

THEN SWEET SALLY and I were caught in a second floor room of the mill, the mill covered with countless tiny shakes, as if fastidious pygmies had worked on the exterior walls.

"This is pretty well exactly why we don't allow no women around," the night watchman said, looking Sally over, measuring her up. Her tiny ribs. "Like with ships," the night watchman added. "No women allowed."

"Women aren't allowed on ships? Well, how do they get anywhere? How did they get from England and Europe to this fair country? I mean, they're here. Did they leap?"

"Now that I can't tell you," admitted our night watchman.

"Maybe they have special distaff ships," I suggested. "To allow travel is what I'm saying."

"It's a strong belief that it's bad luck," insisted the night watchman.

"Well, this is news to me about the ships," Sally murmured, "but of course it must have some sound basis in fact and logic."

LIGHTNING SHATTERS A GIRL and I walk hours of music. Our local brass band celebrates some ribald occasion outside The Elephant Hotel, our raw faltering orchestra in the road, two drums, including a big bass drum and a smaller tom on a belt, sticks bouncing on the dented skins, but no snare drummer, we need a snare, that slurred tidy sound — we all know the snare inserts drama, tension.

AN OLD MAN PLAYS wild clarinet inside the wide flowering horns, big bells of tarnished brass dented and green, held by serious men in angled hat brims. Their repertoire of stiff, wooden marches — they do what they can, they are playful. The different instruments are at odds, yet pushed together, the songs ground up like a pill in an upstairs room, a song with a bad leg, a song like Sally's mouth grazing my ear. Certain moments feed the glutton in me. I'm not convinced this is a terrible thing.

ON OUR LAST hike together we can smell the sulphur springs pressed out of the mountain rocks. Am I going to the middle of hell? A stream falls from on high; it is held above all winter, now the water is free to shatter on the rocks and cliffs. All summer I hold her, but she doesn't always hold me back. I can gauge such things.

She has ribs and a ship has ribs. Sally says, "This is a train wreck waiting to happen. How many people know about us?" This is an example of bad fraught.

LIGHT DIES IN white hours. Sally's hand mangled in the mangle, no hospital built yet. The *Daily Times* reports a crazy man in the vicinity of High Street roaming about entirely naked with the exception of a sheepskin girdle in which is fixed a knife. He is said to live in the woods.

I MAY BE going crazy. I am crazy about her. I cross rude boards over mud torrents, brown worlds moving down our smudged street, the brand new street eroding already, brand new creeks carving their way, the raw road a complete wreck. Our favourite gimp Jonathan falls with a thump, rump stuck in mud and calling out to me in a yoo-hoo falsetto.

"Here, let me help you," I say, but my feet won't move in the gumbo.

"Nah, just leave me here. What the hell."

A gang of hotel women laughs at us. Sally with her bandaged hand pushes me over in the mud and chants in my ear a Liverpudlian seafaring song:

I spent that night with Evangeline, too drunk to roll in bed.
Me watch it was new and me money it was too,
And in the morning with them she fled.

"Oh she can sing like a lark can she not?!"

"Hats off, gentlemen!"

"Women, women," cries the cripple happily, "Oh, I can't stay away from youse, oh my jewels of the alley, my Aphrodite and Demeter, my Hebe and Venus, oh my soiled doves. Hear me, Jezebels, let's jump the broomstick right now. Help me, help me rise or I will water the street in my tears! Only I appreciate you, help me up and I will tear into you, I'll take all of you right now!"

"Say *please*," insists Sally from the dry boards.

TRAINS CHUGGING AND blasting atop blunt creosote ties and tiny metronome birds pecking horse manure. The racket of hammering all day on new side streets, a bakery, a bar, new wood oozing sap, new walls, a barber whistling, a forge roasting horseshoes and banging sparks, new blocks and false fronts, hammering a flimsy town together quickly, another found rhythm, more noise.

SILENT AS GHOSTS, whitetail deer hide with the crazy man with the knife in his sheepskin girdle, pressing the grassy secret lairs and draws, the heights and depths. I step on them and deer leap out underfoot. Years flattened into rocks, years broken out of rocks, frost heaves breaking layers of slate and granite and moss. Sometime during the night of eons the green furry hill came down and curled an arm around sand-coloured boulders, held them.

It's a holy ghost building, Sally sings. But will it ever be finished?

IN THE HOTEL'S gamey gin mill, men, without moving a muscle, wave their sorrows like flags around their heads.
    "What is your opinion of eggs?"
    "The bad ones can be most dangerous."
    "You hungry? Tell him to send us some oysters."
    "He don't have any damn oysters."
    "Well I want some now!"

"You catch more flies with honey than vinegar."

"But *why*. Why would I want to catch flies?"

HORSES RUN AN August evening, a big honey moon held in clouds over the river and hotel and the moon drives under the river and summer lightning at the same time in distant battleship clouds, a weird effect, a light show in the sky, no clear borders, much of the sky in patches of light, shades of white and dark, dark India blue. I can see bright flashes working inside clouds, force, power traded, tested, above and beyond things leap and crackle, like a skirmish in the hills nearby, like sails and dark trees above the red planet.

BILL SAYS, "Why did that woman grab my nose so bold? She laughed at me after. Oh the look on your face, she said. *Oh the look*! I wish there were a few more women in this territory."

"There are other ways, arrangements some men have. At the logging camp one man puts a scarf on and they dance with him for entertainment."

"Men in the logging camp?"

"Some do more than dance I tell yas. In southern European jurisdictions I'm told on good authority that they make a distinction: they say you're only a pansy if you're receiving, not if you're giving."

"Southern jurisdictions and distinctions be damned, who you calling a goddam pansy!"

IN THE ELEPHANT HOTEL trying to stop a fight over words uttered, over nothing, I am clubbed, receive a bevelled angle of bottle glass in my eye. Which side are you now? The half blind side. Forget your history, something vanished, has my eye vanished? The eye weeps, apologizes. Get over it, the eye in love with beauty. My clear cheek cut open, but I can see, I think I still see. I see that love can be deceptive, harmful, beautiful, that I am wedded to my brittle anger and the past is killing me bit by bit, like a series of postage stamps. We get life first in miniature, then we receive it in full scale, ready or no. Or the other way around. But I am okay.

A GIRL VISITING the village is killed by lightning; no warning and she is limp, lifeless. Her body is there, but she is gone. People lie flat all over a field; there were picnics, games, a good crowd wearing gay bonnets and fedoras, but of the mob only she dies. She is the chosen one.

"Please let's do it," I beg. I am a beggar.

"There's no time," she says. "I have to go."

So quiet before, and the lightning and thunder smacked at the same time, one odd cloud moving in over the skinny church, but those at the picnic said they had no hint of danger. Sally and I see the lightning, with no idea it is killing someone, a young girl-woman.

The girl is not even from here. Her family lets her visit briefly and she dies.

Her mother and father will always hate the mention of this village, this county.

WE LIE ACROSS the river from the lightning strike, just another couple in a hotel room. She said earlier that a touch or two is all she needs, she's been waiting, and she is right, only a touch away; she goes off at the same time as the lightning strike; I push into her and see the flash like welding, purple light stuttering in our riverside yards and windows. I hear the instant thunderclap and remark on it.

"That was close," I say.

"That was good."

We are half asleep, I start drifting off, knowing nothing, lying on an oak floor by a pine door. What I merit versus what I receive; this I can never decide. Sometimes I feel lucky, sometimes cursed.

"How is your eye?" Sally asks sleepily.

I love sleepy voices, sleep.

"That scar suits you," she says. "Walk me home?"

Walk me out in the morning dew, she used to sing, not knowing I was listening.

"Say please."

Everyone thinks I am flippant, but I value every second of every second. I do.

IN THE FIELD everyone lies flat, then people stand up slowly. The girl doesn't stand up, something in her stopped by the celestial blow. Lightning went through the girl, nothing personal, simply seeking the ground – she was a conduit, she was in the way. They go to her where she lies, a lethal congregation at her body, a man's voice in panic, a woman, their voices rising on the clumsy river like geese honking.

I IMAGINE THE lightning bolt's electricity funnelled in tiny lines, lintels and openings, a door, power held or moved about in utter mystery, like gaslight, like water forced through straight pipes or crooked branches, delivered as if ordered, designed, needed: *here it is, boss.*

Not what I ordered, suggests the pale dead girl.
My hand brushes her; I want more; I ask for too many things.

Don't, she says, flinching, sensitive to touch afterward.
The girl from elsewhere lying on the field after the blast, lying in her long white dress, her slim legs there underneath; I see her legs, like being inside a tent, festive, sneaky.

WE LIE IN our room; we feel guilty when later we hear the news of the girl. I worry I'll be hit by lightning, be punished because this is so great. In the field they all stand save the chosen one. There are no traces later, it's over.

No, there must be a few traces. Always something.

March weather is mad. I remember my wife's arching back, her form filling my eye, the energy, private parts and the moment's private inventions. We were so close. I saw myself as from a distance, as in a curved lens. I would always be distant, kept at a distance.

"I drink too much with you," my wife insisted later.

ACROSS THE RIVER they lie flat on the field and one girl doesn't rise up (arise ye wretched of the earth). In The Elephant Hotel men play their worn cards, their obedient stories. That time her husband was watching and maybe they arranged it; maybe they talked about it. Sally kept kissing me on the green eiderdown and she held me inside her and he lay down behind her without a word and she moved a leg and he slid in as well, me at her belly and him at her lovely round backside, our two cocks meeting in that one small space with just room for me, no room at the inn, but there he was like another generous finger, Old Adam, and all three of us came in a small interior explosion. For her to have both of us there seemed almost normal, though I have never thought myself cut out for such tricks and we didn't ever talk about it, as if it hadn't happened.

OF COURSE WITH sex there is always another person in the room, sometimes more. Your history and who and where and what you remember, all those people in the bedroom with you.

I remember that Sally went back to him and his books and yellowed receipts. He was a mild little fellow who drank, and most thought there was something lacking and she deserved better, but she found some comfortable music in him.

"A quiet conscience sleeps through thunder," Sally says to me. "A quiet conscience," she says, "is like a soft pillow."

SKITTERING GRASSHOPPERS DROP on our wells and crops and orchards; I think of the Bible and the garden in ruins. Sally is losing her religion, but goddamn, it keeps coming back like a bad penny. She slips and falls on the crushed locusts, their squished juice like grease on the ground. Her fall and she wrecks her wrist and knee.

"I'm pregnant," Sally says when I visit one afternoon. He is absent, selling a good leather saddle he inherited. "From that night, so I don't know which of you. Maybe both. That can happen; it's a fact."

OUR LAST DAY we wash inside a bright river, swallow tender salmon and wild grainy honey. The sun pours on us, no lightning at our heads. My hand on her. I want to go on. I can't stop myself. Am I a glutton, a predator, a parrot, a fool? The glacial water, Tom's a-cold. I am catching flies. Wasps also. She prefers *him*. Fuck fuck fuck. All day I think about us. It has to be *us*. Someday I'll catch up on sleep.

THE NARROW PATH past Mount Zion becomes a track, then a corduroy road, then cabins and chairs and stables, clearings, pale meadows in dark piney woods. The constant sound of axes. Giant trees become stumps, become gaslight shadow and heaps of smoking ashes and eggshells become posts and planks. Fields of green grain spring from the ashes.

One lane, two lanes. Two eyes, one eye. A duet becomes a solo.
You did not hear no young girl crying.

"When will I see you?" I ask for no reason. Why do I open my mouth?

"I just don't know," she calls miserably from her walls of meds and dandelions and caveats. "I wish it wasn't so complicated."

Wooden wheels grind splinters and hooves clop past debtors and dissembling drummers and drovers, bulky garlic eaters and spies and flower sellers walk on, andante.

SALLY'S MELANCHOLY MUSIC no longer at my ear. The quiet. Some days I hate the hornet drone that thrives in my head, I want the vespiary to be still – yet some days I need a distracting universe of noisy notes and melody.

WALK ME OUT *in the morning dew*, Sally sang, not knowing I was listening. I will lift a red accordion from the unquiet rooms of Slovakia, at dawn I will wander roads the colour of figs past the mumbling chained convicts and the world's wooden hotels and mills' ravenous saws and past her house and her grey cracked trees held horizontally in a staggering snake fence. I know where they keep the petty cash. I will continue.

OUTSIDE CAMP, PAST the leaking white tents, I watch as three wildcats are evicted from their soft tiny dens – aromatic tunnels of light heaving open as heavy pines go down, wildcats snarling mad, felines trilling in a surly exhalation of natural notes, open notes. She went back to him and his yellow receipts.

They flee from me, and the big cats flee down a raw road in the stumps, crossing small lit clearings, their rear end wildcat cadence bobbing through dark reaches and pine slopes under the violent music of my old hand-fiddle, my double-headed axe.

WHEN WILL I *see you?* Why do I open my mouth when I know every answer already? I keep walking.

In the silent morning animal tracks tiptoe our river shore and rushing rivers with their contract to drain our cloudy dream landscape.

HARRIS GREEN BELOW THE CHRISTIAN SCIENCE READING ROOM

This pretty town I lived in long ago. I wish to walk miles down to the water. Buoys clang as boats sail in front of mountains, cliffs riddled by surf where curious seals watch yoga poses held eternally on polished cedar decks. Now that I am back, this world of mandated lawns and lush plants unnerves me.

In an air-conditioned grocery gentle Tunisian techno plays and my jaundiced eye and I spy aisles of organic arugula, ginger aioli, probiotic kambucha, and a cheery sign:

Wellness is not a Fad – It's a Lifestyle!

These lovely grocery aisles are a spec-script of our fears: some serial killer just past the door we can stave away with a payoff, shelling out cash for detox teas, sea-salt cleanses and spas, antioxidants and scalpels.

In the AC grocery I pay for a pretty sandwich and walk out into sunlight, walk slow miles downhill to the harbour. Passing Harris Green, I see a man trying to stand, balance just not there. Call him Stagger Lee. Beside Stagger Lee a man sits on a bench with no head, decapitated by his king or his T-shirt pulled over his head to trap a cloud of smoke to his face, to optimize the smoke, lit rock and tiny chalice hidden under his shirt, *get it all*, draw every wisp of the wreath and heavy is the head that wears the crown, that lights the lighter.

Gazing over the narrow park is the Christian Science Reading Room, its Georgian curves and glowing pillars a marvel worthy of Venice or Dublin.

Katie the poet told me her ex-boyfriend, during a period of mental illness and marginal housing, was clubbed over the head in Harris Green; his skull cracked and he nearly died from his brain swelling in its shell. Remembering Katie's story, I keep to the park's edge, speed-walking as if my head might catch a contagion (*it's not a fad*!).

Katie said, "Zeke was living in one of the flophouse hotels downtown, sink in room, shared bathroom at end of hallway. Zeke walked with a wooden cane that had a pretty carved duck's head atop, and someone whacked him over the head with his own weapon. The assailant was a homeless guy; he had his own set of problems. Zeke went into a coffee shop for help and behind the counter they told him he was bleeding heavily from his forehead, but they didn't give him any help."

Katie says she hasn't gone by recently, but she hears the area is gentrifying, condos bunged in everywhere, higher rents and fewer tents. Today among the condos Stagger Lee tries to stand by his headless friend, tries to stand, but ends up dancing a little jig like Adolf by the Paris railcar.

On Harris Green citizens seem less concerned with wellness than what I saw in the AC grocery aisles. Like antiques, these faces show *honest wear*. Harris Green shaves life to fewer factoids, a rock, a gram, a grim belief in magic and lustral transactions involving lighters.

Katie said, "I went to see Zeke in the hospital. They had to saw out part of his skull and his head was half-shaved: staples on one side, long stringy hair on the other. It was pretty sad: already suffering from schizophrenia and now a brain injury on top of it. You know, I feel a bit iffy on the ethics of telling you his story."

Way out there white sails cross the strait and on slant rocks fat sea lions bay like bloodhounds. Real estate on the west coast is hot. *Their* hot real estate is this scruffy park, a few shopping carts piled high as wagon-trains dreading a salt plain, the crossing.

How many cross over from this little patch of ground? Fentanyl and carfentanil: a hotspot the size of a grain of salt can kill you. Like Fortinbras' army, they are not afraid to die for a straw, an eggshell, though this Stagger Lee army has trouble just balancing.

I wonder if anyone is reading *Hamlet* in the Christian Science Reading Room? Its pretty dome hovers over the park like a whitewashed skull. Hey, mixed feelings about killing a rat or a king? Forget all about it here. Need a week in an all-inclusive? Problems with IT and that Drombo-Western deadline? Such matters have no place in Harris Green.

No green tea or yin yoga in the park, but a strangely effective fitness plan, not an ounce of fat. These are citizens sans water view and Filipino nannies, sans tax lawyers and lawn mowers and no need for the TCM wine club. A life stripped of weight, sanded down to the *Repeat* button, iterations of one musical riff, a grain of rock, Blake seeing the world in the weight of a grain and the weight of a soul sailing free of a body like smoke.

Such admirable jeweller-focus, one true faith instead of a dozen false idols; they are true to themselves and to erasing themselves while a nervous ambulance waits beside the park to create their death.

Katie said, "From the coffee shop Zeke made it to his hotel; a resident found him unconscious in the communal toilet and was smart enough to call in paramedics."

On occasion the ambulance siren and lights fly our street to give us a jolt, a flashing mime show of grief's rocket. The Queen says Hamlet is fat and has a blond comb-over. Among these poor shades I should be a plump target, my skull next to be cracked, but they don't see me. I am the ghost on the ramparts; it's my world that is no longer real, I'm a figure on a lunar rock past the edge of planets, past the edge of focus.

Distant glass mountains form blurred monuments to our smoking forests, our lifestyle, our summer of fire and ash and bloody lingering moons. This headless man holds his private smoke under his T-shirt, his fire, his investment in property. Feed your head, delete your head, take this from this, take this communion.

And where stands Christ the Scientist in this calm mayhem? Science: some users are genius scientists, canny chemists, like my old neighbours on Crease Avenue, discovering ways to extract a high from a tire or blade of grass. Bootface, Gold Car Guy: can they still be alive?

Lacking charity, I grew to hate those puking addicts and jonesing prostitutes crossing my yard, wanted to kill the dealer next door with piano wire. I was influenced by the 1960s, thought I was non-violent and disliked authority, but on Crease Avenue I learned I lean toward violence and preferred the sight of the bumbling SWAT team and their joyous dogs, got to know them well.

"Zeke was in the hospital a long time," Katie said. "He got the chunk of skull replaced, but had to wear a bike helmet until his head healed up."

Steppenwolf sings, *You don't know what we can find*, and in the Dakotas they find they can hoover fuel from rock, splintered lessons in shale gas. Chinese factories feed us fentanyl and carfentanil in the mail. The bells of the sea ring out past the safe harbour, but no swimming sirens appear to Zeke or to Stagger Lee and the body of his headless buddy.

Once women bathed in the river and my eyes lingered on Teresa's body, her skin; we were cold and pure; we went back to the land in our pearl button shirts and roughout cowboy boots. I painted Fred Radomski's barn for his buckskin jacket. Our lost summer of mescaline picking fruit by easy lakes. Sprinklers came on in the night to drive us from the park and, baptized by whirling dervishes, we rose to drag our sodden sleeping bags to the dark beach.

The Youngbloods and Steppenwolf sing on the car radio, but on Harris Green the magic carpet ride is not going so well. An ambulance has so many tiny windows and an eagle with a habit flies over the condos to peck at your liver. Your body opened; does an emoji exist for, *Hey, they cut out a chunk of my skull?* An ambulance at Harris Green like a food truck waiting on its best customers. It's not a Fad – It's a Lifestyle.

Blue straits roil, snowy peaks rise above us; in ancient worlds seafaring kings and spies dreamed such blurry visions. Out on the water, past the periodic table and cold tides, sea lions moan on rock islets, sombre as Grubski trombones, and Belgrade to Botswana, every rental car preset to classic rock. Our orchards on fire and we crack shale to combust a rich intersection of ingredients in our smoking chalice.

NOWHERE MAN'S SECOND DAY AT THE RUINS

T hunder and lightning reverberate over the ruins of Pompeii and our nervous hotel dog opens his jaws and speaks to the sparking sky. Loose dogs lope everywhere and outside the pink hotel we sit in wicker chairs and watch the stone street and marvellous dogs and sky.

The wild dogs running free make Tamika jumpy. We walk to the central piazza and dogs trot out of nowhere, surrounding us as we search for bank machines that might like us.

"Damn! That's not right!" Tamika exclaims. "Where are all these dogs coming from?" Looking all around. "I don't like this."

Finally one machine accepts me, pours euros into my hands, and what joy, connection and love after so many rejections. The world works, will let me keep buying drinks for Ray-Ray our disgruntled singer and Tamika who plays keys. We depend on machine after machine.

All the trains in the gloaming and buses in plumes of diesel beneath olive valleys and aqueducts and trefoil arches. Our group on the move like vapour, up and down, back and forth over roses and skeletons, crowded platforms and subterranean stairs and sweaty carriages under the looming volcano and cactus and lava fields once taken for portals to hell.

The sweltering train circles the volcano, the volcano always looming in the window, sea on one side, volcano on the other.

Ray-Ray the singer makes a point of talking with any other Blacks he sees in Italy. He grabs my arm outside the train station, asks me, "Where is *nowhere*?"

"What do you mean?"

"Those guys I just talked to say they live in nowhere."

"They're homeless? They live on the street?"

"No! A place, man, they say they live in nowhere."

Nowhere? I have to think about this.

"Way up north, man, they say it's a good place, I should come visit."

"It's a country up north?"

"Yeah, man, way up there."

"Norway?"

"Yes, man! Nowhere! It's a good place. Here they treat me like a dog, I may go up and see Nowhere. I don't dig it here in Italy." Ray-Ray lowers his voice. "In fact, I think I'll leave tomorrow," he says in a confidential tone.

"Give this a chance."

"Man, they liked me way more in China."

Tamika says, "They thought you were NBA."

"Well they don't like me here in Italy."

We move in such crowded cities and on crowded trains, yet see so many empty valleys between the cities, between Naples and Rome. Millions of Italians crammed into projects and slums and yet so much open country just out the door, just down the road.

I suppose it is the same everywhere. We don't want *Lebensraum*, we don't care for the apple orchard by the stream. We gravitate to cement cities, born there or moving there we follow our bliss, follow our desire for the hustle of slums and stairwell rats and staple-guns and opiates, love to hang out at the curb or line up for bonehead jobs and pick each other's pocket and live without leafy trees or pink blossoms, our desire to avoid God and nature, to take groaning elevators to boxes set atop boxes, our desire to stand on each other's head to the soundtrack of machines and synths.

Yesterday Ray-Ray said he didn't feel right. "Man, I feel sick; maybe I caught something in China or on the plane."

"How you doing today?" I ask.

"Man, thank you for asking. I could be dying and that dude running this show doesn't care."

Ray-Ray says he is leaving the band. "I've had it, man. I'm leaving tomorrow." Tamika ignores him. We'd be in trouble without a singer, but Ray-Ray threatens this every day. I'm a bass player, I'm nobody; but we need a singer.

Our second day at the ruins. A dog runs and jumps in the distance.

In this heat the dog gallops after pigeons in the grassy ruins of the Grande Palace; rows of ancient pillars and amputated stubs hint of the ordered space where nobles roamed gardens and temples.

The dog cares not a whit about us or human history or the future, it cares only for the moment and the nearest pigeon. The dog is running full speed when I arrive and running full speed when I leave. Tongue hanging in the heat, the creature pants manically, a clicking sound.

Tamika asks, "How does the dog find water here?" Pompeii is a dusty desert.

An Irish boy jumps away nervously as the Jack Russell rockets by, running at a pigeon he will never catch.

"Mom, what's that dog doing?" The Irish boy looks scared.

The dog runs over lava and candy wrappers and king's tombs. The dog turns back and runs again, over and over. That woman in Canada, I must change her mind, I must swim with her again.

A tiny corpse lies in the thick dust, lies flat as a comb.

"Is that an antique rat?"

"Yes, dear," says the boy's mother. Antico.

"Can I have a fizzy drink?"

"I already said no! Don't start up. Not another word about fizzy drinks!"

All the worn-out parents, all the offended children. Everyone on tour is frazzled, thirsty. Slaves and emperors and gladiators ate the same Italian dust that ruins your camera. Place this ancient soil in your mouth like a thick piece of pizza pie and eat the rich past. Dig anywhere in Italy and find the past; you can't escape it. Tamika and

Ray-Ray and I must leave these ruins, leave this skin that is sore from the burning sun.

I have never sweated like this. A shantytown burns below a freeway and I know I could drip my endless sweat over the class-war conflagration and extinguish the flames. I'm sure our collective sweat will pool on the floor of the train until our ankles are deep in sweat, in aqua vitae, the saltwater of life.

Naples at night – I can still conjure the scent of crazy Vespas and heaped garbage and brilliantined pickpockets.

PULL OURSELVES FROM a mattress at dawn for another woozy train to Pompeii's sun-bright ruin, and Napoli in sore shoes to climb a thirteenth century alley of cobbles and skewback abutments and dodge speeding scooters in a lane narrow as a closet and wolf down the best pasta ever and pizza that is almost liquid. What devilish alchemy makes their food so delicious?!

The train station where I last saw the Texan woman makes me feel like a loser, Napoli station a sad axis. It was so fast and gone: her promise, her name in all the stirring names, Pompeii, Herculanum, Sorrento, Amalfi, Positano, Napoli, and soon we will be back in the bosom of peach-coloured Rome.

I buy a ticket, another machine, and we climb on the last train and down the aisle. I take a seat on the right. Ray-Ray takes a seat on the left side of the aisle.

Ray-Ray says he is the second son of the second wife, so his status in Nigeria is lower than the eldest son.

Ray-Ray says to me, "Bet you five euros no one will sit by me."

I've gotten to know Ray-Ray on the road; he chases all the Croatian chambermaids and is a bit of a con man, but really he is a creampuff. At a party he worried I hadn't eaten and deftly cooked me seafood and rice. But he is so tall and so dark. The Italians fear him.

"Will you take my bet?" Ray-Ray asks me. "Five euros."

Sure, why not. Someone will sit by him.

The seats around me fill up, the train to Rome fills. The feeling of pure will as the train shunts from the station and I lose my five euros bet to a new form of Jim Crow, every seat occupied except for three blue seats around Ray-Ray.

Avenues in Rome seem so familiar, pleasing after Napoli's volcanic dust and volcanic drugs and jackal-headed bedlam and mountains of stinking trash and that sharp knife in Napoli steering its casual way through the air of a kitchen party. We ran down the stairs like athletes.

Naples is compelling, stranger than Rome, a fascinating paella, but Rome seems a kind of home now, a comforting feeling since I have lost my home, lost my way.

In Rome I check e-mail and my spam: *I am Mrs. Stella Ethan, a Christian. I have picked you for an inheritance. Everything is available.*

How I love that last phrase; it sounds so simple.

Well, Mrs. Stella Ethan, I'll tell you: I wish to drive a Hupmobile, an azure Nash Metropolitan, a whisper slide ride past the riding stable to park at my home by the well-behaved sea: *Hi Honey!*

And Stella, please note that Moorish window across the street, a modest but beautiful place. My desire is to buy that whitewashed building, make it my home. Maybe I'll add an art deco cinema and a blind pig, an illegal bar with rounds on the house when the Pope drops by, and our band will open for Amy Winehouse on that tiny stage in the corner.

In this lovely foundling world all thirsty dogs shall have water and machines will pour out euros and Mister Jim Crow begone forever. Have confidence, all of us happy together in the blue seats, bad tattoos removed, our teeth restored, riding into heaven beside peasants and messiahs.

Mrs. Stella Ethan the Christian calls from my spam folder. Have confidence! Accept my proposal in good faith, she says. Everything is available, Stella says, and why would we doubt her heart-warming words?

ABOUT THE AUTHOR

Mark Anthony Jarman is the author of *Knife Party at the Hotel Europa, My White Planet, 19 Knives, New Orleans Is Sinking, Dancing Nightly in the Tavern*, and the travel book *Ireland's Eye*. His novel, *Salvage King, Ya!*, is on Amazon.ca's list of 50 Essential Canadian Books and is the number one book on Amazon's list of best hockey fiction. His *Selected Stories* is forthcoming from Biblioasis Press.

Mark won a gold National Magazine Award in nonfiction, has twice won the Maclean-Hunter Endowment Award, won the Jack Hodgins Fiction Prize, was shortlisted for an Atlantic Book Award, the Alistair MacLeod Prize, the Thomas Raddall Prize, was included in *The Journey Prize Anthology* and *Best Canadian Stories*, and short-listed for *Best American Essays* and the O. Henry Prize. He now teaches at the University of New Brunswick where he is fiction editor of *The Fiddlehead* literary journal.